WITHDRAWN

Henry Holt and Company, *Publishers since 1866*
Henry Holt® is a registered trademark of Macmillan Publishing Group, LLC
120 Broadway, New York, NY 10271 · mackids.com

Our books may be purchased in bulk for promotional, educational, or business use. Please contact your local bookseller or
the Macmillan Corporate and Premium Sales Department at (800) 221-7945 ext. 5442 or by email at MacmillanSpecialMarkets@macmillan.com.

Library of Congress Control Number: 2021047593
First edition, 2022
Book design by Ashley Caswell
Printed in China by Hung Hing Off-set Printing Co. Ltd., Heshan City, Guangdong Province

ISBN 978-1-250-14274-0 (hardcover)
1 3 5 7 9 10 8 6 4 2

When colors fall in love,
they decide to mix.

Together, they create new families.

Families that play together,

eat together,

disagree with each other . . .

. . . and celebrate together.

But sometimes . . .

And then **everything** changes.

But after a while,
bit by bit . . .

. . . the colors start to feel like themselves again.

Life is so vibrant!

The colors still worry.

But with open minds . . .

. . . love . . .

...grows.

Life can be even
better than it was before!

Families don't always stay the same.
Sometimes, they

REMIX!

. . . to create a new beginning.